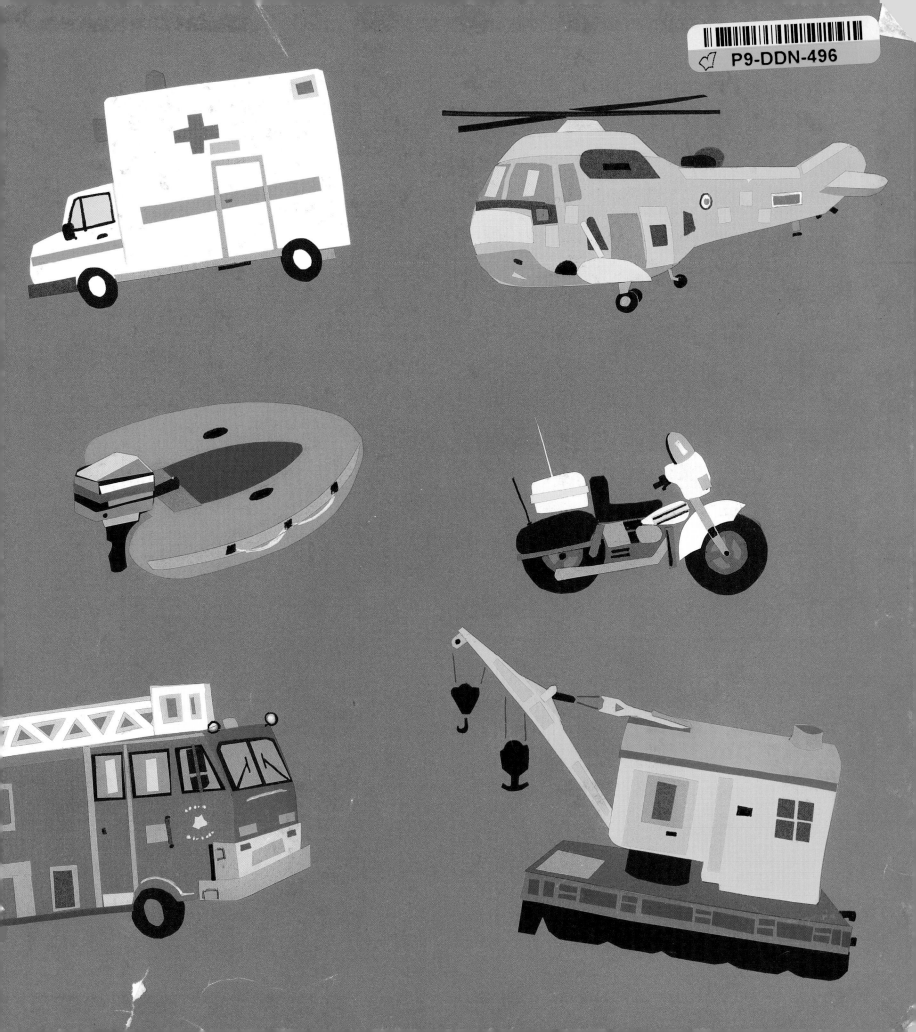

For Ann and Michael
MM

For Marcus, Michelle, and Jay
AA

First American edition published in 2002 by Carolrhoda Books, Inc.

Text © 2002 by Margaret Mayo
Illustration © 2002 by Alex Ayliffe

Originally published in 2002 by Orchard Books, London, England.

Carolrhoda Books, Inc.
A division of Lerner Publishing Group
241 First Avenue North
Minneapolis, MN 55401 U.S.A.

Website address: www.lernerbooks.com

Library of Congress Cataloging-in-Publication Data

Mayo, Margaret.
    Emergency! / by Margaret Mayo ; illustrations by Alex Ayliffe.
       p.   cm.
    Summary: Rescue vehicles race to help during a variety of emergencies.
    ISBN: 0–87614–922–0 (lib. bdg. : alk. paper)
    [1. Emergency vehicles—Fiction. 2. Safety—Fiction. 3. Stories in rhyme.]
  I. Ayliffe, Alex, ill. II. Title.
  PZ8.3.M457 Em 2002
  [E]—dc21   2001006951

Printed and bound in Singapore
2 3 4 5 6 7 – OS – 07 06 05 04 03 02

GENCY!

written
by
**Margaret
Mayo**

illustrated
by
**Alex
Ayliffe**

🍃 Carolrhoda Books, Inc. / Minneapolis

Call 911—emergency!
Burglars make a getaway.
Police car dashing, bright lights flashing,
Help is coming. It's on the way!

Ambulance needed—**emergency!**
Whee-*oww!* Whee-*oww!* Pull over, make way!
Lights beaming, sirens screaming,
Help is coming. It's on the way!

Tree on the track—**emergency!**
A rescue train will clear the way.
Huge crane hooking,
lifting,
shifting,
Help is coming. It's on the way!

Boat sinking fast—emergency!
Launch a lifeboat into storm and spray.
Ropes tossing, life preservers dropping,
Help is coming. It's on the way!

Traffic jam—emergency!
Police motorcycle speeds down the highway.

Zipping, revving, redirecting,
Help is coming. It's on the way!

Forest fire blazing—**emergency!**

Fire-fighting planes zoom up and away.

swoop, swoop, swooping, water scooping,

Help is coming. It's on the way!

River flooding—emergency!
Inflate the rafts without delay.
Supply boats tugging, chug, chug, chugging,
Help is coming. It's on the way!

Blinding blizzard—emergency!
Snowplow moves the snow away.
Pushing,
shoveling,
tossing,
tunneling,

Help is coming. It's on the way!

Fire! Fire—emergency!
Fire engines race all the way.

Hoses rushing,   water gushing,

Help is coming.
It's on the way!

Hiker lost on mountain–emergency!
Whirr! Whirr! Helicopter hovers and sways.

Searching, finding, side door sliding,
Help is coming. It's on the way!

Uh-oh! Accident—emergency!
Damaged car blocks the way.
Tow truck towing,
           yellow light glowing,
Help is coming. It's on the way!

All quiet now—no emergency.
The rescue vehicles are all tucked away,
Ready and waiting for the next 911 call.
Then help will be coming to save the day.